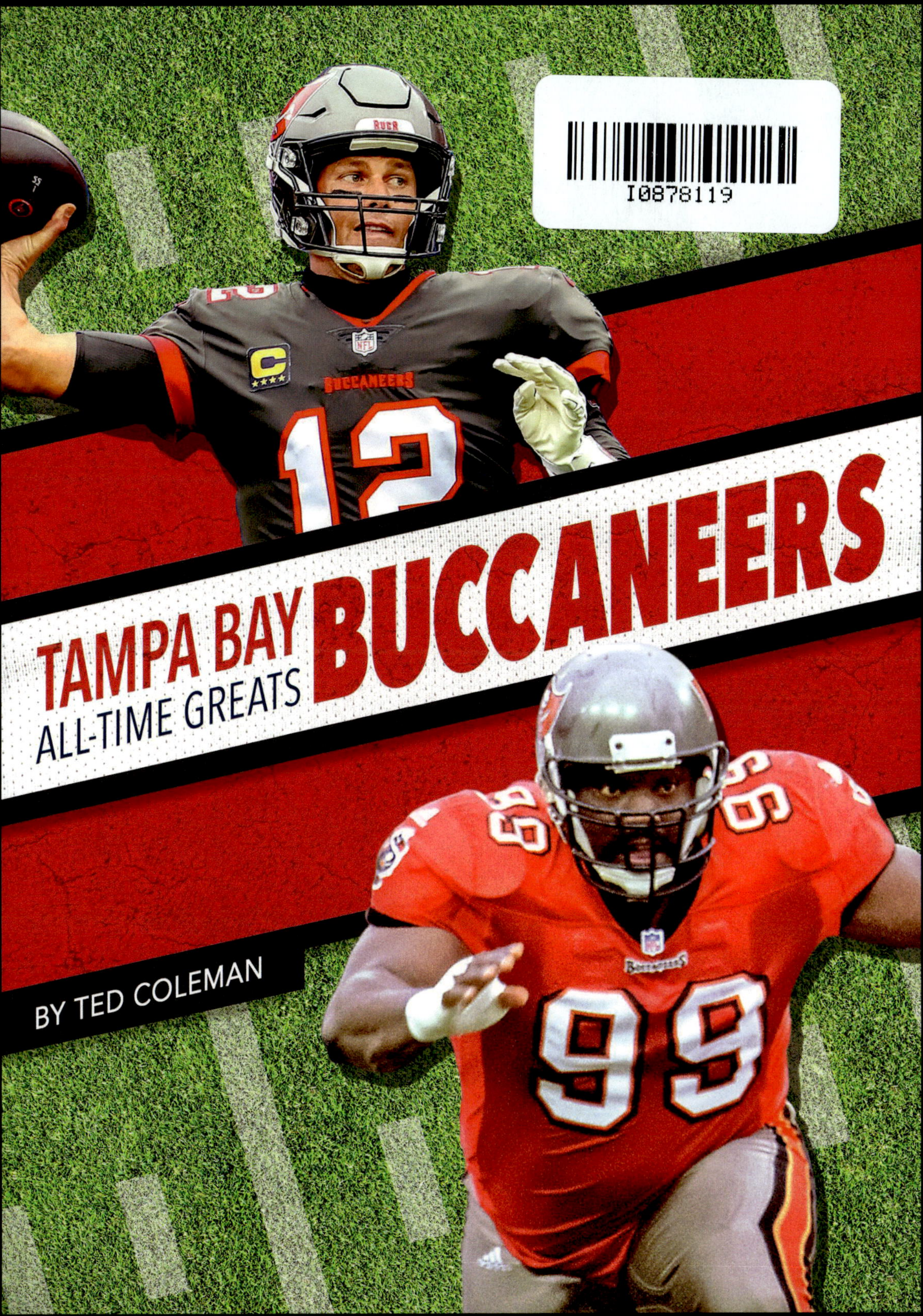

TAMPA BAY BUCCANEERS

ALL-TIME GREATS

BY TED COLEMAN

Book design by Jake Slavik
Cover design by Jake Slavik

Photographs ©: Mark LoMoglio/AP Images, cover (top), 1 (top), 18; Tom DiPace/AP Images, cover (bottom), 1 (bottom), 13, 21; Peter Read Miller/AP Images, 4; Al Messerschmidt/AP Images, 7, 15; Vernon Biever/AP Images, 9; David Durochik/AP Images, 10; Chris Gardner/AP Images, 14; Allen Kee/AP Images, 17

Press Box Books, an imprint of Press Room Editions.

ISBN
978-1-63494-367-3 (library bound)
978-1-63494-384-0 (paperback)
978-1-63494-417-5 (epub)
978-1-63494-401-4 (hosted ebook)

Library of Congress Control Number: 2020952636

Distributed by North Star Editions, Inc.
2297 Waters Drive
Mendota Heights, MN 55120
www.northstareditions.com

Printed in the United States of America
082021

ABOUT THE AUTHOR

Ted Coleman is a sportswriter who lives in Louisville, Kentucky, with his trusty Affenpinscher, Chloe.

TABLE OF CONTENTS

SELMON
63

CHAPTER 1

BUILDING A WINNING TEAM

The National Football League (NFL) came to the Tampa Bay region of Florida in 1976. But winning did not come with it. In their first season, the Tampa Bay Buccaneers lost every single game. And in their second season, they lost the first 12 games.

Defensive end **Lee Roy Selmon** was there for those dark times. But he also helped turn things around. In 1979, the Bucs notched a winning record for the first time in team history. Better yet, they reached the playoffs. Selmon was Defensive Player of the Year that season, and he made his first Pro Bowl. He would end up going to five more Pro Bowls during his Hall-of-Fame career.

On offense, the team's leader was quarterback **Doug Williams**. Williams had a cannon for an arm. He had no trouble throwing the ball deep. Williams was also tough. During his rookie season, he played one game with a broken jaw.

Williams had one huge weapon on offense. It was tight end **Jimmie Giles**. In the 1970s, most tight ends were

QUARTERBACK STRUGGLES

Before and after Doug Williams, the Bucs struggled to find a star quarterback. Their first starter, **Steve Spurrier**, didn't win a game all season. Fans had high hopes for **Vinny Testaverde**. He was the first overall draft pick in 1987. But Testaverde threw more interceptions than touchdowns in each of his six seasons with the Bucs.

known for blocking. But Giles could also catch and make big plays. In 1979, he caught the game-winning touchdown as Tampa won its first-ever playoff game.

A later piece of the offensive puzzle was running back **James Wilder**. He was a powerful runner who wasn't afraid to smash into defenders. Wilder helped the Bucs make it back to the playoffs in 1981 and 1982. Then in 1984, he exploded for 1,544 rushing yards. Wilder ended his career as Tampa's all-time leading rusher.

When Lee Roy Selmon retired after the 1984 season, the Bucs needed a new leader on defense. Linebacker **Hugh Green** stepped up. Green helped start a tradition of linebacking excellence in Tampa.

STAT SPOTLIGHT

CAREER RUSHING YARDS

BUCCANEERS TEAM RECORD

James Wilder: 5,957

The next great linebacker was **Hardy Nickerson**. Known as "Hardware," Nickerson came to the Bucs in 1993. He brought hard hits and leadership to the defense. The Bucs were not a good team during most of those years. But players like Nickerson helped them build a future winner.

SAPP
99

CHAPTER 2
THE FIRST CHAMPIONS

Head coach **Tony Dungy** joined the Buccaneers in 1996. Dungy was known as an excellent defensive coach. And defense was what eventually made the Bucs champions.

Tampa's next great linebacker was **Derrick Brooks**. Brooks was strong and tough. He never missed a game in 14 years. He also made the Pro Bowl in 11 of those seasons. Brooks recorded more than 1,700 tackles during his Hall-of-Fame career.

Warren Sapp anchored the defensive line. Sapp was a fierce pass rusher. He also had a big personality, and he was known as a team leader. Sapp spent nine seasons with the Bucs. During that time, he recorded more sacks than anyone in team history.

Defensive end **Simeon Rice** was a consistent pass rusher. He recorded double-digit sacks in all but one of his six seasons with Tampa.

The secondary had a pair of legendary players. Safety **John Lynch** was known as one of the hardest hitters in the game. He also had great field vision. Lynch made 23 interceptions during his 11 seasons with the Buccaneers.

STAT SPOTLIGHT

CAREER SACKS

BUCCANEERS TEAM RECORD

Warren Sapp: 77

LYNCH
47

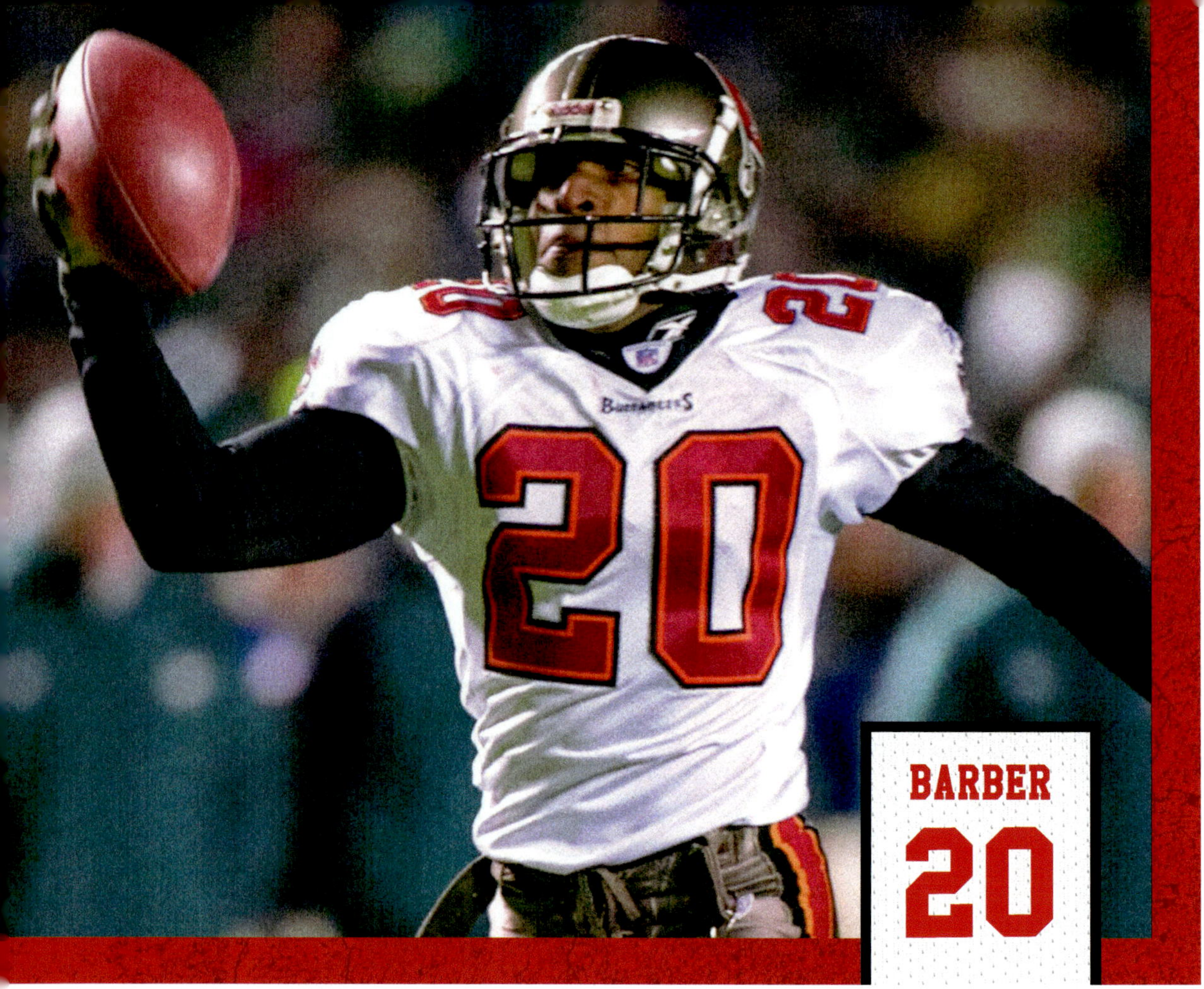

Cornerback **Ronde Barber** had great vision, too. He racked up more interceptions than any player in Bucs history. And from 1998 to 2012, he didn't miss a single game. That set an NFL record for most consecutive games by a defensive back.

The Bucs weren't all about defense, though. Quarterback **Brad Johnson** was a veteran player. He wasn't flashy, but he didn't make many mistakes. Johnson had played on several winning teams before joining the Bucs. He was just the player to lead Tampa's offense.

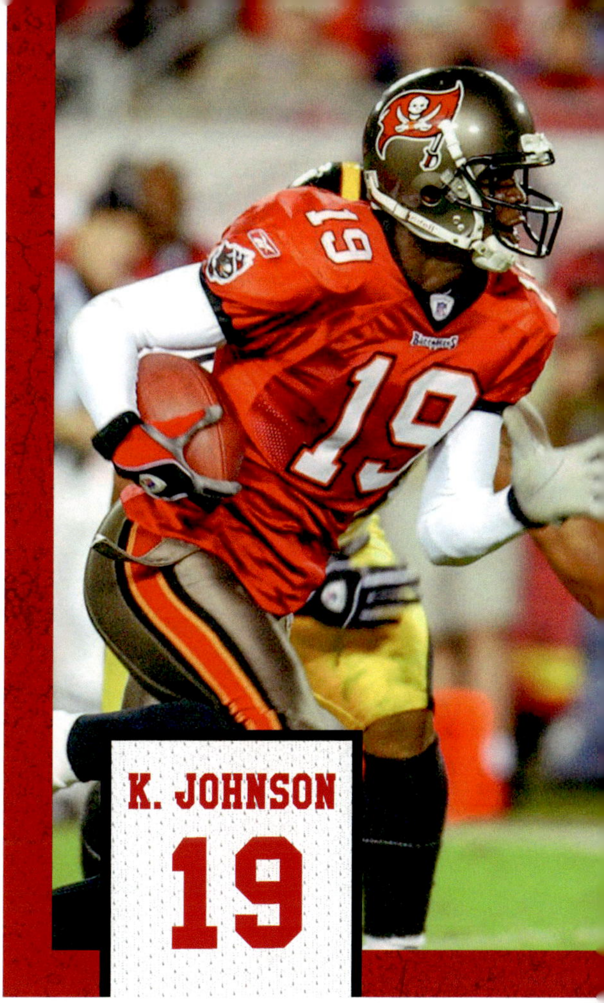

One of his favorite targets was **Keyshawn Johnson**. The star receiver was one of the most exciting players in the league. With his speed and height, he made plenty of big touchdown catches.

The Bucs also had a steady fullback in **Mike Alstott**. Most of the time, Alstott used his bruising body to block. But when he got the ball, he could gain tough yards. Alstott played his entire 11-year career in Tampa. He finished second on the team's list of rushing leaders.

The Bucs got a new head coach in 2002. **Jon Gruden** maintained the success that Dungy had built. The Bucs were finally Super Bowl contenders. They had Pro Bowlers at every level of the defense.

In the 2002 season, the Bucs faced the Oakland Raiders in the Super

TAMPA 2

One of Tony Dungy's biggest impacts was his defensive system. The Cover 2 defense uses two safeties playing deep. Dungy's variant became known as the Tampa 2. It dropped a middle linebacker deep into pass coverage. This system became a popular defense in the NFL for years.

Bowl. Safety **Dexter Jackson** was not one of Tampa's best-known defenders. But he made two of the biggest plays in team history. Jackson had two interceptions in the Super Bowl. He earned Most Valuable Player (MVP) honors for the game. Tampa won the first championship in the history of the franchise. And the 2002 Bucs defense became known as one of the best ever.

BRADY

12

CHAPTER 3

THE NEXT CHAMPIONS

The Buccaneers went into another decline after their Super Bowl victory. In 2015, Bucs fans thought they had a new star quarterback with **Jameis Winston**. That season, Winston threw for more yards and more touchdowns than any rookie in team history. But he also threw too many interceptions. Winston was gone after the 2019 season.

In 2020, an NFL legend became available. **Tom Brady** had already won six Super Bowls with the New England Patriots. When he joined the Bucs, he instantly made them a contender.

Many of Brady's passes went to receiver **Mike Evans**. Evans was Tampa's all-time leading receiver. In fact, he recorded more than 1,000 receiving yards in each of his first seven seasons.

Once again, the Bucs also boasted a great defense. Linebacker **Lavonte David** was a powerful run stopper. Fellow linebacker **Devin White** was a top pass rusher. And linebacker **Shaquil Barrett** added to that fierce pass rush. Tampa's strong

BRUCE ARIANS

Bruce Arians spent five years as the head coach of the Arizona Cardinals. He retired after the 2017 season. But the Bucs brought him back in 2019. Arians assembled a talented group of assistants. He hired former NFL quarterback Byron Leftwich to coach the offense. Meanwhile, Todd Bowles coached the defense. At the age of 68, Arians became the oldest coach to win a Super Bowl.

defense carried the Bucs through the playoffs and to the Super Bowl.

In the big game, Brady did what he came to Tampa to do. He made the Buccaneers champions. The Super Bowl victory left no doubt that Brady would be remembered as one of Tampa's all-time greats.

TIMELINE

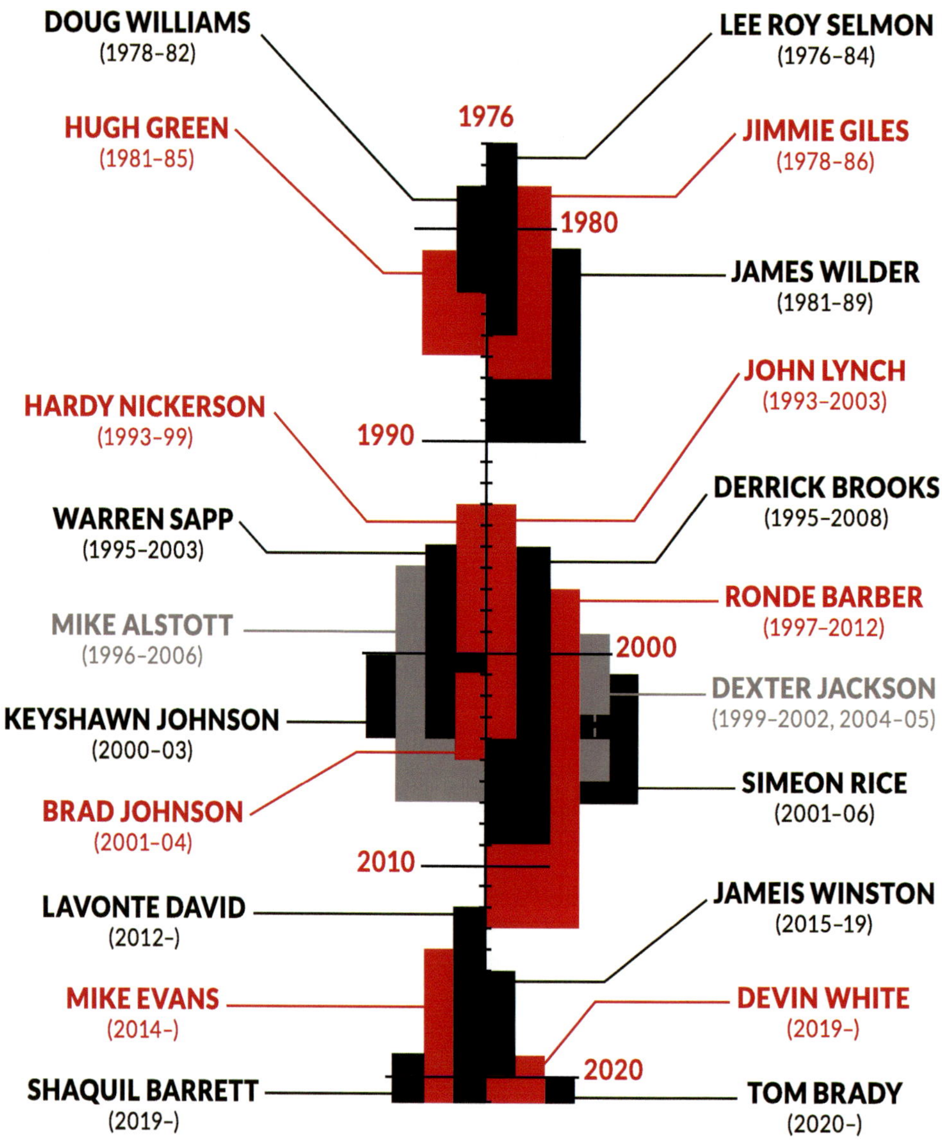
DOUG WILLIAMS
(1978–82)
LEE ROY SELMON
(1976–84)
HUGH GREEN
(1981–85)
1976
JIMMIE GILES
(1978–86)
1980
JAMES WILDER
(1981–89)
JOHN LYNCH
(1993–2003)
HARDY NICKERSON
(1993–99)
1990
DERRICK BROOKS
(1995–2008)
WARREN SAPP
(1995–2003)
RONDE BARBER
(1997–2012)
MIKE ALSTOTT
(1996–2006)
2000
DEXTER JACKSON
(1999–2002, 2004–05)
KEYSHAWN JOHNSON
(2000–03)
SIMEON RICE
(2001–06)
BRAD JOHNSON
(2001–04)
2010
LAVONTE DAVID
(2012–)
JAMEIS WINSTON
(2015–19)
MIKE EVANS
(2014–)
DEVIN WHITE
(2019–)
2020
SHAQUIL BARRETT
(2019–)
TOM BRADY
(2020–)

TEAM FACTS

TAMPA BAY BUCCANEERS

Founded: 1976

Super Bowl titles: 2 (2002, 2020)*

Key coaches:

Tony Dungy (1996–2001), 54–42–0

Jon Gruden (2002–08), 57–55–0,
1 Super Bowl title

Bruce Arians (2019–), 18–14–0,
1 Super Bowl title

MORE INFORMATION

To learn more about the Tampa Bay Buccaneers, go to **pressboxbooks.com/AllAccess**.

These links are routinely monitored and updated to provide the most current information available.

1966 through 2020

GLOSSARY

contender
A team that is good enough to win a title.

cornerback
A defensive player who covers wide receivers near the sidelines.

defensive back
A cornerback or a safety. These defenders typically cover wide receivers.

linebacker
A player who lines up behind the defensive linemen and in front of the defensive backs.

Pro Bowl
The NFL's all-star game, in which the league's best players compete.

secondary
The defensive players who typically cover wide receivers.

veteran
A player who has spent several years in a league.

vision
The ability to see how a play is developing and to know what will happen next.

INDEX